Undercover Assassin

By M.s. Rose

Table of Contents

About The Author 4

The New Beginning 5

The Wake...7

The Past Life 10

The First Assignment 13

The Challenge 17

End Challenge 20

The Investigating 23

The Rundown 26

The Race..29

Storytime..32

Ready or Not..38

Ready or Not P2 44

Back to Reality 48

NOTE FROM THE AUTHOR 50

About The Author

M.S. Rose emerges as a compelling new voice in YA contemporary fiction, crafting stories rich with emotional depth, authenticity, and heart. Her writing explores identity, resilience, and the moments that shape who we become, speaking directly to readers navigating the space between who they are and who they are becoming.

When she isn't writing, she's off on badass adventures—chasing unforgettable experiences, indulging in amazing food, and soaking up life alongside the people she loves most.

The New Beginning

There is a girl named Mazikeen. She's an 18-year-old black girl with ginger hair; she's very athletic and has hazel eyes. Mazikeen has just started her senior year at a new school in a new state. She thinks she has gotten a fresh start, or so it seems.

Over the summer, while Mazikeen settles into her house, she makes two close friends. Scarlet and Ash are also roommates. Mazikeen gets a text from Scarlet one summer day asking, "Hey, let's all go to the African Zoo, it's Friends Day, so Ash is coming."

Mazikeen texts Scarlet, saying, "See you then at the African Zoo."

They see all different types of animals and go on a gondola to see around the whole sanctuary. After an exciting day, they go home.

By the time everyone gets home, it is nighttime, and everyone goes to bed. Mazikeen keeps tossing and turning in the middle of the night until she decides to get up and go for a walk.

She walks down the street, trying to clear her mind. She can't help but feel that soon something will take away her new happiness.

While she walks down the street, hands in her pockets, head down, she hears footsteps coming behind her, followed by a gunshot. Bang!! Then everything goes... dark.

The Wake

Mazikeen jolts awake, finding herself in the hospital. She looks down and sees bandages, then feels a burning sensation and an ache in her right shoulder. Mazikeen sees a clipboard at the end of her bed, and she leans forward carefully to reach for it.

As Mazikeen reads the charts, she learns she was shot in the right shoulder. "Well, that'll explain the bandages and the sudden feeling in her shoulder," she thinks to herself.

She continues to read more and notices she has been in the hospital for weeks now, since that night. A nurse, a curvy Latina about 5'5" with jet-black hair, comes into the room, looks around, and charts something without saying a word. The nurse starts to walk to the door and stops in the doorway to say, "A man is waiting for you outside."

"What man!?" Mazikeen tries to ask, but the nurse shuts the door. Mazikeen takes a breath, grabs her clothes—that are sitting in the black office chair next to her—and gets dressed.

As Mazikeen starts to walk towards the outside hospital doors, she sees a very tall man, about 6'4", leaning against the wall with his sunglasses, hands in his pockets. As she gets closer, he starts to look a little familiar. When she gets outside, she looks and sees that it's Father. He smiles as if he is supposed to be there, as if he hasn't been gone for 6 years; as if that incident hadn't changed their life, and she had to leave it all behind.

Mazikeen asks Father, "What are you doing here?"

"I came to talk," Father says.

"Who said I would talk to you?" Mazikeen says as she walks away from him.

"I did, so let's talk," Father says firmly as he grabs her arm and pulls her to him. Mazikeen jerks her good arm away; she thinks to herself, "He's probably the reason I got shot."

In spite of that, she says, "Don't act like you did nothing wrong, there's no need for you."

Mazikeen walks towards the parking lot. *(Skttr)*

A black SUV jumps in front of her. "Get in the car."

Father pushes Mazikeen into the backseat before she can move. After Mazikeen gets pushed into the car, she sees Father's minions, Danny and Chris.

Father starts to drive away from the hospital, going to who knows where. Danny and Chris stare at Mazikeen with big eyes, and their jaws drop.

"What's wrong with them?" Mazikeen sarcastically says to Father.

"Well, the last thing anyone knows is you're dead, Mazikeen," Father says while keeping his head straight. The words cut deeper than the bullet wound.

Dead? She freezes, pulse racing, as if the world has just erased her existence without her consent. They shake their heads.

"How's the new life?" Danny asks, smirking. Danny is close to her age. She's 20, Mexican, has black butchered hair, brown eyes, is 5'0", and has a vine with thorns tattoo on her left arm.

"Yeah, are you finally normal?" Chris finger-quotes and laughs. Chris always thinks he is funny, but he is not. He's a little older, 22, white, blue eyes, 5'6", and has the same vine with thorns tattoo on his left arm.

Mazikeen looks away and sits in silence, gazing out the window. Mazikeen thinks to herself, "He must have told them what I did. Back when my name wasn't Mazikeen, when I went by Black Lotus."

The Past Life

This all started long ago when Mazikeen was a 5-year-old girl. She is found in a snowy back alley of a restaurant and taken in by the top Russian Assassins. The assassins are code-named Father and Mother; they took Mazikeen because they want to make her the Top Undercover Assassin. For 7 years, they train her to be at the top of her class and how to execute until the very end.

Mazikeen is 12 years old now. This is the day that she has been preparing for, the day she gets her first assignment, the day she gets to choose her code name. This little girl runs down to the headquarters office. She gets to the grand double-oval mirror, wooden doors and pushes it open to see Father and Mother standing, waiting... for her. The girl sees five old, wrinkly men in black satin suits and ties, wearing black theater masks that hide all their faces except their mouths. In the center stands a man draped in red velvet, his mask grotesque with three faces fused into one, each expression frozen except for the blood-red mouth.

"This young lady has come here to see us today, because it's the day. The day of her life when she gets the chance to choose."

The Head of the Red Veil stands, opening his arms in an inviting gesture. "Now," the Head Councilman says as he points to another council member.

"Give her the divine list, for she gets the honor to choose her name. The name she will be feared for, the name that will be legendary, the name she will be known as forevermore."

The Council member hands Father the list. The little girl grabs the list, trying to keep her excitement under control. The little girl keeps her eyes glued and runs her finger down the list, looking and scanning for a name until her finger stops... and her eyes stay glued. Her finger stops trembling at one word. 'Black Lotus.'

The syllables root inside her, dark and elegant, like petals opening to drink in the shadow. Father and Mother always call her their little lotus flower of darkness, for she inevitably incinerates items to their very charcoal core.

She walks over to Mother and tells her the name she chose.

Mother relays the message to the Head Councilman. The Head Councilman looks over the Council of the Red Veil, then nods toward the little girl to signal their acceptance.

He rises, scanning the room before proclaiming, "This young lady shall now be known by the fearsome name... Black Lotus!"

Applause erupts as Black Lotus is welcomed into the Red Veil's assassin ranks.

After a moment, the Head Councilman glances at Father and Mother, signaling that their part in the ceremony is complete. They offer one final nod of pride before exiting the chamber.

"Now," the Head Councilman says as he returns to his seat, "It is time."

He looks to the Council.

"Let us grant Black Lotus her first assignment."

The First Assignment

"For your first assignment, Black Lotus, you will kill a girl named Asya White," the Head Councilman says, while a Councilman hands her the target's information. The document shows a picture and reads, "Asya White, 21-year-old girl, fair skin, Russian, with curly black hair, kind brown eyes, 5'5"."

"Kill her, what for?" Black Lotus asks.

"She is a threat that needs to be taken care of. Are you up for the job?" the Head Councilman asks with a seeming glare. Black Lotus nods and heads towards the door.

"One thing," the Councilman mentions. "You can't breathe a word about any of the assignments to anyone. Not even Father or Mother."

"Understood," Black Lotus says and walks out

the door. Black Lotus goes to the weapon quarters and starts gearing up for the car that leaves in 3 hours.

Black Lotus looks at herself in the mirror and sees the blank expression on her face; all the excitement has left her body as she thinks to herself, "I'm ready."

"Black Lotus?" A tall, black-haired, white, long, slinky man in his 30s walks towards Black Lotus.

"Yes?" she responds.

"Follow me to your car," he says as they walk towards a limo-style car. Black Lotus nods and walks towards the door of the car.

"I am Mr. Bell, your personal driver," he says while opening the door for her. He is about 6'0" and has sunglasses on the whole time. She acknowledges what he says and gets into the car. He drives to Kirov, Russia, where Asya White lives. They get into the city and see Asya walking on the street. The driver keeps driving and turns the corner a block down. Black Lotus gets out and heads into this abandoned building, where all her equipment is set up and ready.

Black Lotus gets into place, and a few minutes later, Asya walks into the coffee shop across the street. Black Lotus watches and studies Asya for hours as she meets up with friends, reading a book and drinking her coffee. Asya finally wraps up her visit and starts to head out.

Black Lotus grabs what she needs, heads out of the abandoned building, and heads towards the crosswalk to cross the street. After Black Lotus crosses the street, she is only a few feet away from Asya.

Asya is heading home, walking in the snowfall, bundled up in her brown coat. Asya then hears footsteps behind her and looks to see if someone is walking behind her, but no one is there. Asya quickens her pace, the crunch of snow echoing louder than it should. Each glance over her shoulder reveals nothing but darkness, yet the dread in her chest swells with every step.

Walking faster and faster, looking behind her, Asya turns the corner of an alley, trying to take a shortcut, and runs into someone, falling on her butt to the snowy floor.

It is Black Lotus, a 12-year-old little girl. "You gave me quite a scare there," Asya says as she grabs for her chest and chuckles, for she is trying to catch her breath and calm down. Black Lotus smiles and reaches out her hand to help Asya up from the snowy floor. Asya grabs Black Lotus's hand and gets back on her feet. Black Lotus pulls out her knife and stabs it into Asya's stomach.

Asya looks down at her stab wound and back up at the little girl, speechless as she falls back onto the snowy ground. As it looks like Black

Lotus is going to leave Asya there to bleed out, Black Lotus pulls out her silencer and looks Asya right in her face with the same blank expression she had before. All of her innocence and joy end here as she shoots Asya between her eyes. Black Lotus puts the silencer away, pulls out her phone, and presses the star (*) key. Black Lotus's car from before pulls up, and she gets in, leaving Asya's body in the alley.

When the car gets back to the Institution, she walks up to the Head Councilman in his office and throws the file on the table in front of him. Then she walks towards the doorway. Before leaving, Black Lotus stops and says, "Next time, give me a challenge." Then she leaves the room.

The Challenge

A few months have passed since the first assignment. Black Lotus has made her way up the ranks to become one of the best assassins. She knows she can become the best if she just keeps pushing herself.

It is Friday night, and on Fridays, the mentors go on what they call "date night." She starts thinking, "They won't come back until Monday, and with new assignments for a selective few. However, I know it's the time everyone leaves their 'unit' and does what they think is fun for themselves, whether it's with the person they are partnered with or with the one they want to sneak off into the night."

It is that night tonight, and Father and Mother are gone. Black Lotus is called up to HQ; she makes her way up there and is told she has another assignment. Black Lotus opens the grand double-oval mirror wooden doors to see the Head Councilman and the other Councilmen. Black Lotus walks to the middle of the room.

"An assignment," the Head Councilman says as a greeting.

"Of course, sir, what's the assignment?"

"A challenge," he says with a smirk. "Just like you asked." He hands Black Lotus the assignment folder.

The name blurs on the page: Star-Fire. Her throat closes, breath jagged. For a moment, she wonders if this is a mistake, a cruel test. But the folder in her hands feels like a death sentence.

"What is this!?" Black Lotus asks, confused and angry.

"The next target, what else would it be?" the Head Councilman says with a straight face.

"This is crazy, why kill her!?" she thinks as the anger grows inside of her.

"She is working for the other side, selling all of our secrets to them," the Head Councilman starts to explain.

"She would never!" Black Lotus starts.

"Well, she has, now she has to go. Do your assignment or face the consequences of the Red Veil."

Black Lotus collects herself, nods, and walks to the quarters for her equipment.

Black Lotus gets to the quarters, and an assistant is there to help gather the equipment. They see Black Lotus' face and ask, "Is everything ok?"

"Yes, everything is fine," Black Lotus responds with a dead tone. The assistant gives Black Lotus the equipment, and Black Lotus leaves for the plane.

As Black Lotus sits in her seat, she starts thinking, "Should I go through with this, should I face the consequences…?" The Head Councilman gave her a challenge for sure with this assignment, but that's what she asked for.

Two days later, Black Lotus lands in New York City, USA. At the moment, that is where the target is. Black Lotus heads into the hotel room to set up and stay out of sight from the target, for they know each other.

End Challenge

After a day of following the target, Black Lotus is still in disbelief.

"Selling secrets to the other side," she thinks. The Councilmen aren't right. Now that Black Lotus has made a decision, it's time to put an end to this target, no matter how hard it will be.

The target leaves their room to do their thing, and Black Lotus prepares for the execution.

At 11 pm, the target comes back to the room to find Black Lotus sitting in their hotel room chair, waiting in the dark for them. The target turns on the lights and jumps, ready to attack, only to see Black Lotus sitting there. "What's this?" the target asks.

"Don't play dumb with me," Black Lotus says, sitting legs crossed and a silencer in one hand.

"So they found out about the other side?"

"Why? Why go to the other side and destroy everything our people do!" Black Lotus says as she starts to stand.

"You wouldn't be under..." Black Lotus slaps the target with the back of her gun before they can finish explaining. Black Lotus raises the silencer, looks the target in the face and says, "Goodbye, Mother."

Bang!! Bang! The silencer goes off twice.

Mother falls to the floor as a tear runs down her cheek, and she takes her last breath. Black Lotus leaves the room, never to see Mother again.

Now Black Lotus has landed back at base and goes up to HQ to see the Head Councilman and to debrief. When Black Lotus gets up to HQ, she sees Father standing waiting.

"How was the assignment?" Father says with a weird grin.

"What's the meaning of this? Where is the Head Councilman, and where are the Councilmen?" Black Lotus says while walking up to him in confusion.

"Hand over the file," Father reaches.

"Out!" Black Lotus shouts.

"Only the person who assigned the assignment

can obtain it," Father says, smirking, with his hand still out, waiting for the file.

Black Lotus's expression hardens as she finally connects the dots: Father gave her the assignment; Father killed Mother.

Black Lotus throws the file on the floor in front of his feet. Black Lotus turns around and heads for the door.

As she is leaving, the Head Councilman walks into the room. The Head Councilman sees Father and Black Lotus in the HQ office and yells, "What's the meaning of this?!"

No one answers him.

The Head Councilman walks up to Father and notices a file on the floor. He bends down and grabs the file. The Head Councilman sees the attached photo; it shows Mother with a big, fat, red X. The Head Councilman yells for security to come and take Black Lotus away, but before they can, Black Lotus pushes right through them and runs to the quarters to grab her equipment.

As Black Lotus gets there, an alarm goes off, and she knows she's limited on time and grabs what she can, what she thinks she needs. Black Lotus takes off, never to be seen by the agency again.

The Investigating

Mazikeen shakes her head from the memory of what happened back then, to see that Father has stopped on the side of the road.

After a few moments, he gets back in the car. "Why have we stopped?" Mazikeen asks.

"Need to drop something off," Father says. The minions start grinning ear to ear as they get out of the car with ginormous bags.

"Mazikeen, keep a lookout!" Chris says.

"Look out for WHAT?!" Mazikeen yells as they close the trunk.

"What else?" Danny says, opening her door. Danny opens the bag, showing the bars of gold, pearls, and jewels. "It's called a drop point, now watch." Danny pushes Mazikeen out of the car.

Mazikeen can't shake the feeling about her shooter still out there, and now she is being put into a scheme she has no idea about. In the unfortunate events, the cops are coming down the street.

Before she can alarm everyone, the cops see the car sitting on the side of the road and the enormous black bags. The cops grab them and take them down to a small-town station for questioning.

When Mazikeen gets to this small brick building with wooden benches, they sit her down. The cops call them one by one, and while Mazikeen waits to be called, she thinks about what to say.

First Chris, then Danny, and after they finish, they are able to leave. As the last person, Father returns, walks towards Mazikeen, and sits down.

Father tells her, "Don't say anything about what happened out there, remember the code." Father then gets up and walks out the door.

"Mazikeen," a male cop calls out. Mazikeen walks towards the room the cop is guiding her to and sits down. The officer closes the door behind Mazikeen. Another female officer is sitting there, waiting for them to take their seats.

"Someone got shot a few nights ago. Have you heard of it?" the male cop asks, taking his seat.

"I was shot a few nights ago," Mazikeen thinks. It was her. "No, I haven't," Mazikeen says.

"Well, how was the hospital visit?" the female officer asks. It's surprising they ask her about that, but they would know they can look up records.

"Why are you asking me these questions?" Mazikeen asks.

"You should really be asking about Father and the minions," Mazikeen thinks to herself.

"Just trying to see what information you know," the female asks.

"Do you have a reason to detain me?" Mazikeen says, getting ready to leave.

"No, you're free to go." The male cop gestures to the door. Mazikeen gets up, walks out of the interrogation room, pulls out her phone, and Uber driver.

Once Mazikeen gets to the door, Father and the minions are standing outside waiting for her; she gets into her car and leaves them behind.

The Rundown

Mazikeen sees her best friend, Scarlet, walking down the street on their way into town. "Pull over here, Sir," Mazikeen asks, but the driver keeps driving. Mazikeen's eyes keep on Scarlet as she disappears into the distance. Mazikeen sits back down in her seat and acts like she wasn't ignored. The driver then steps on the gas, and they start going faster and faster. Mazikeen realizes that this isn't her Uber driver.

"What's the rush?" Mazikeen asks calmly.

"No rush," the driver responds just as calmly. The car veers onto the sidewalk, smashing tables, scattering mailboxes, and tearing through anything unlucky enough to be in the car's path. Then the car goes up a flight of stairs.

"What's going on!?" Mazikeen screams as soon

as the question comes out of her mouth, and they crash into the side of a two-story building. They fall all the way down to the first floor, leaving both the driver and Mazikeen unconscious.

A few minutes go by. Mazikeen jolts up and crawls out of the car, stumbling to open, holding her arm and looking up at where they fell from. Mazikeen then clutches her arm, white-hot pain surging through the old wound. The scar never fully healed, and now it is tearing open again at the worst possible moment.

The driver just wakes up and crawls out of the car on the other side.

Mr. Bell yells, "I'm sorry."

"For what!? Almost killing me!?" Mazikeen yells back.

"For not finishing the job," Mr. Bell says as he starts running towards her. Mazikeen takes off running. Where will she go?

She runs up the escalator and onto the second floor. Mazikeen looks back as she runs and sees a new body running behind Mr. Bell.

That person yells, "I will shoot you if you don't stop running."

"Do it!" Mazikeen yells back.

"You want to hurt all these people?" The mystery person says sarcastically as they shoot an innocent bystander. Mazikeen wants to stop, but she knows if she stops now, she will be killed.

Bang! Another shot goes off, and this time it is Mr. Bell falling to the floor. "Get out of my way!" The mystery person says, running past the body.

Mazikeen can't get distracted; she has to keep running, and so she does, until the mystery person yells, "Enough of this!!" They shoot into the air, breaking the glass above where Mazikeen is about to step. Mazikeen stops immediately.

"Now stop running, wouldn't want to be shot again now, would you?" The mystery person says with a ginormous grin.

"Hands up and turn around slowly." Mazikeen is hesitant, but she puts her hands up and slowly turns around.

"Who is this person?" Mazikeen thinks to herself. Once Mazikeen turns around and gets a good look at the mystery person's face, she sees it is none other than Dreux... her sister, code name Evil Sister.

"Dreux?" Mazikeen yells.

"Yes, it's me, hello sister. I was the one who shot you, Councilmen's orders," Dreux yells back to Mazikeen, still having her gun pointed at her. Dreux was the one who shot Mazikeen that fateful night; she's the reason her whole past has come out to play these last few days.

"Now to finish the job. Goodbye, Black Lotus." Bang! ... a gunshot is heard.

The Race

Bang! The gunshot splits the air, echoing in her skull. Mazikeen looks down and grabs her clothes. Dreux's gun is still pointing at Mazikeen, but her gun didn't go off. Mazikeen looks at Dreux and sees that Dreux has been grazed on the ear by another gunman. Dreux looks for the person who shot her and shoots at the person.

While Dreux is shooting, Mazikeen tries to escape, and as Mazikeen is escaping, Dreux turns back around and shoots Mazikeen in the same spot as that night. The other gunman shoots Dreux in the hand, making Dreux drop the gun. Mazikeen looks up and sees one of Father's minions.

"Run!" Danny screams, and Mazikeen takes off.

Before Mazikeen is out of sight, "Every second you waste bleeds your friends dry," Dreux sings, her voice sharp as glass. The words burrow into Mazikeen's chest worse than the bullet wound. Mazikeen flies through the double doors, thinking, "It is only a matter of time before someone gets to her friends. Well, let's see who gets there first."

As Mazikeen runs, she bleeds all over her clothes, but she doesn't care because she needs to get there first. She needs to save her friends! Mazikeen runs into Scarlet's house and finds her in the kitchen.

"Scar!" Mazikeen yells.

"Hey Maz, where have you…"

Scarlet finally closes the refrigerator door and sees the blood dripping through Mazikeen's hands while she's holding her arm.

"OMG, what happened!?" Scarlet asks, rushing to grab towels and the first aid kit.

"No time, we need to leave!" Mazikeen says, walking into Scarlet's room. Mazikeen pulls out a black backpack from Scarlet's closet, packed and ready to go.

"Why? For what?" Scarlet asks. Mazikeen pours alcohol and patches up her shoulder.

"What the heck is going on!" Scarlet says in a panicky manner.

"Get packed now!!" Mazikeen says firmly. Scarlet grabs a bag and starts to pack. Mazikeen changes her clothes, grabs her backpack, and heads to the living room.

"I'm ready," Scarlet says. *vroom*

Bullets start flying into the house. Scarlet screams. They scurry behind the kitchen island; Mazikeen grabs her throwing stars and guns from the hidden compartment.

"What now, Mazikeen?!" Scarlet asks while ducking her head from the stray bullets.

"We need to get out of here and find Ash; he isn't safe anymore," Mazikeen says while giving Scarlet a mask. Mazikeen then throws tear gas out of the window and towards the gunmen.

As soon as Mazikeen does, Scarlet and Mazikeen run as fast as they can to Scarlet's car. As they get into the car, Mazikeen sees Evil Sister ready for battle but just missing them. And off Mazikeen and Scarlet go.

Storytime

"Where is Ash?" Mazikeen asks Scarlet.

"Ash should be at the school; he said he was tutoring."

Mazikeen calls Ash and says, "Ash, I need you to grab your things. We need to leave. I'll be there soon."

Mazikeen pulls up to the front of the school, and Ash is there, standing outside with their backpack.

Ash gets in the car and asks, "What is going on, Mazikeen?"

"Not now, it isn't safe for you guys here anymore."

"No, Mazikeen, tell us now! We were just shot at. I need to know why," Scarlet yells while grabbing the steering wheel.

"You've been what?!" Ash yells. Mazikeen pulls over and puts the car in park.

"There are really bad people coming for you guys because of me, now I have to finish this once and for all." Everyone is silent. Mazikeen puts the car in drive.

After a few moments, "We're here for you, Mazikeen, whatever you need," Ash says, putting his hand on Mazikeen's shoulder.

"I just need to get you guys to a safe place first," Mazikeen says, stepping on the gas.

15 mins later. Mazikeen, Scarlet, and Ash finally get to the safe house, and everyone gets out of Scarlet's car.

"What is this place?" Scarlet asks, closing the car door.

"This is a safe house, for whenever they would come for me," Mazikeen says, putting in the code for the door, then opening it. Once they walk through the doors, it looks like a regular house.

"This way." Mazikeen gestures to Ash, and Scarlet looks at each other and walks down the slender halls into a bedroom with a single door inside.

"I want to show you something." Mazikeen opens the door to a high-tech, secured room that has a ginormous smart computer, guns, weapons, and so much assassin equipment.

"Mazikeen, tell us what's going on. What is all this?" Ash says, staring in awe at all the equipment.

"Yes, Mazikeen, tell us who these people are," Scarlet asks, looking at Mazikeen.

Mazikeen sighs, "Ok, ok, I'll tell you everything, but you're going to want to sit down for this one." Mazikeen gestures to the chairs behind them. Everyone sits down.

"I'm different than what I seem. I didn't come here with my family, as you know; they didn't die in a car accident. I moved all the way here to get away from him..." Mazikeen says with a distasteful tone.

"What? Who's he?" Ash asks.

"Are you going to shut up long enough for me to tell you?" Mazikeen gives Ash a stern look.

"Sorry," Ash zips his lips with motion.

"Like I was saying, I was adopted by some bad people," Mazikeen says while dropping her head.

"How bad can they be?" Scarlet says, jokingly nudging Ash.

"I was adopted by a Russian Organization called The Red Veil. Two Russian assassins named Father and Mother took me under their wing." Mazikeen's voice strains as she lifts her gaze. Scarlet's hand flies to her mouth; Ash's eyes widen. The silence that follows is louder than any gasp. Their mouths drop.

"When I was 5 years old, my real parents died in some freak accident, and somehow, I was left in an alleyway, and Mother found me. They took me in, and I trained to be the top assassin. When I was 12, they had me train with the pros. I was the youngest in my class, and I had the best scores; that's when they called me to HQ," Mazikeen says.

"Who did?" Scarlet asks, tuned into the story.

"The organization was called The Red Veil and its council. The Head of the Red Veil was the person who gave me my first assignment, my first kill." Mazikeen looks ashamed and ready to turn away, but she sees them leaning in, waiting... wanting to hear more.

"I did the job quickly and easily at 12 years old. I had my first body; I was officially an assassin; I was officially named BLACK LOTUS." Mazikeen's face gets serious; it's about to get deep.

"That's when I went back to the Councilmen and told them I wanted a challenge, a harder assignment, that's what they did. They gave me an assignment I thought I would never have to take. I was assigned to kill Star-Fire.... Mother. Father was the one who convinced the head councilman to turn on her. He was the one who had the assignment bestowed upon me," Mazikeen gasps, disheartened.

"I'm so sorry, Mazikeen, that's a terrible thing," Scarlet says as she and Ash stand up to hug Mazikeen.

"After I found out that he was behind it all, I went to the weapons armory, grabbed what I could carry and left. I left so no one can find me, where I can start fresh," Mazikeen finishes.

"Wow, Mazikeen, that's a lot to take in. But you're not alone," Ash says, grabbing Mazikeen's shoulder.

"You never will." Scarlet grabs them for a group hug. Mazikeen shakes out of the hug.

"No, I can't have you guys come with me to end this. It's too dangerous, it's my fight, not yours."

"Fine, we will stay here as backup." Scarlet clicks her tongue

"Yeah, backup," Ash says while grabbing the equipment.

"Do you know how to work these things?" Mazikeen asks, holding back her laughter. Scarlet and Ash shake their heads yes and then no.

"Here." Mazikeen pulls up the communications on the screen and shows them how to use it and insert the earpiece.

"Ok, now I have to go to a private island. So

there might be a little interference with the coms." Mazikeen changes her outfit to be combat-ready. She grabs her equipment and gives Ash and Scarlet a nod.

"You got this, Mazikeen!" Scarlet says.

"We're here for you." Ash gives a thumbs up. Mazikeen is going after Father, the Councilmen, and the Head Councilman, and she knows exactly how to do it. Now Mazikeen heads off to Malum Island.

Ready or Not

Mazikeen goes over the plan one last time with Ash and Scarlet before getting to Malum Island. Ash and Scarlet are going to help Mazikeen with her goal of taking down Father, the Councilmen, and the Head Councilman.

"Now that we have that set, I'm arriving at the port," Mazikeen says.

"Why do you have to go to the ports?" Scarlet asks over the comms cluelessly.

"I need a speedboat to get to the island," Mazikeen says with a devious smirk. Mazikeen has just arrived at the ports and found her slick black speedboat with red trim. Mazikeen activates the speedboat with a remote phone and begins her journey, her goal to stop everyone once and forever.

It isn't the smoothest ride to the island's shipment ports; Mazikeen rides through this sudden rainstorm, trying to keep her balance and dodging the intense waves coming her way. Mazikeen has reached the island's shipping port. Mazikeen goes around the side to park her speedboat for her later escape. Mazikeen makes sure she isn't seen getting into the building through the shipment ports.

She watches as the guards walk past and sees an opening; right before the doors close behind the last guard, Mazikeen slips right in.

Once Mazikeen is through and passes the guards, she sees an open crate, jumps in, and closes the top. Mazikeen then pulls out a virtual 3D map of Malum Island to see exactly where they are taking her and check in on coms.

After being placed in a dark room for 30 minutes of no movement, Mazikeen opens the crate and hops out. Mazikeen looks around to ensure the room is secure. Mazikeen is in her fight gear: an olive-green cotton crop top, black, sleek gloves, and camo cargo pants.

After clearing the room, Mazikeen grabs her backpack and straps on her amber-colored utility belt. Mazikeen then reaches towards her ear, "Do you copy? Chris?" Mazikeen says quietly.

"Yes, we copy," Chris responds.

"What's my status?" Mazikeen asks.

"You are now clear to move," Chris announces.

Mazikeen opens the storage room door where the crate is stored. She makes sure it is clear; Mazikeen is on the move.

"Ready or not, here I come, Father," Mazikeen says firmly.

Mazikeen stealthily makes her way to the HQ office, knowing that's where Father will be. On the way up, Scarlet asks, "So what is your exact plan when you find Father, Mazikeen?"

"Nothing you need to know, but I can say it won't be pleasant," Mazikeen says forcefully.

"Ok, the next room is good to go in 3...2..1. Now!" Chris says attentively. Mazikeen blows a dart at the first guard and puts the second guard in a chokehold, causing him to pass out. Mazikeen swiftly moves to the next room.

Suddenly, Mazikeen stops in her tracks and sees something she thought she would never come across again, her old quarters where she used to take her classes. "Black Lotus, #1," Mazikeen thinks to herself. She pushes the thought to the back of her mind and keeps moving until she makes it to the door of the HQ office.

The office where she was given her last assignment, THE CHALLENGE. Mazikeen swings open the grand double-oval mirror wooden doors with guns blazing, killing 3 of the Councilmen's men and grabbing the last one as a hostage.

"Come out, Head Councilman, I have your man," Mazikeen says, screaming while holding the gun to the last Councilman's head.

"Ah, Black Lotus, nice of you to join us," the Head Councilman says, coming out from around the corner.

"Where is he!?" Black Lotus yells across the room.

"I don't have the slightest clue…"

"Bang!" The gun goes off, killing the last Councilman of The Red Veil.

"I'm not playing your games anymore," Black Lotus says while letting the body drop.

"Now tell me where he is."

"Well, let me think," the Head Councilman says, trying to reach for the gun under his chair.

"Bang!" Black Lotus shoots at his hand.

"Don't even think about it."

"Father is leaving for an assignment. If you hurry, you might catch him." The Head Councilman steps down in front of the grand council table.

"I'm not done with you yet," Black Lotus says, keeping her guard up.

"Well, let's settle this like adults then," the Head

Councilman says, moving closer.

"If it's a killing you want, then it's a killing you'll get," Black Lotus says, dropping her gun and pulling out her knife. The Head Councilman does the same, throwing off his red satin robe and grabbing his knife, which he had underneath. Then the fight to the death begins. Black Lotus lunges at the Head Councilman first. He dodges the strike and comes at her with a counterstrike, grazing her arm.

"What are you and Father's plans?" Black Lotus asks while touching her arm.

"Why would I tell you that? It would ruin the surprise!" the Head Councilman says with a devilish smirk. Then he runs forward to attack Black Lotus. Black Lotus ducks and tackles the Head Councilman, pinning him to the ground.

"Tell me the plans now!!" Black Lotus yells at the Head Councilman, pinning his body in a scorpion position.

"What would Mother think if she could see you now?" The Head of the Red Veil groans calmly.

Black Lotus shatters the Head Councilman's left kneecap with the back of her knife. "What was the real reason to kill Mother?!" Black Lotus says harshly.

"Father saw others were looking through files that were out of her jurisdiction," he says slowly.

Black Lotus stabs him in his right side, "Talk faster!"

"Father told the Councilmen that brought it up to me. Father claims Mother knew too much of the secret plan and that she needed to be exterminated!" The Head Councilman yells out in pain.

"Why did I have to kill her? Why did you try to take me away? What is the plan?!!" Black Lotus yells as she twists the knife deeper into his ribs.

Out of nowhere, a guard comes up behind Black Lotus. The guard grabs Black Lotus and puts her into a chokehold. The Head Councilman gets up, holding his side and says, "You remind me so much of Mother, it's a shame."

The Head Councilman limps away, making his escape. Black Lotus stomps on his right foot, and a blade comes shooting out the front. Black Lotus high kicks the guard, aiming for his face, making him drop dead.

"Pathetic," Black Lotus says while rubbing her throat. "Chris, Scarlet, find me the coordinates of Father and where his assignment is." No answer. "Chris... Scarlet... come in, do you copy?" Black Lotus heads towards the docks and is stopped by a voice that sounds all too familiar.

"Why in such a rush, don't you miss me... Black Lotus!"

Ready or Not P2

"Why in such a rush, don't you miss me, Black Lotus?!" Evil Sister says sarcastically.

Black Lotus turns around, "Miss you? Ha, don't make me laugh." Black Lotus lunges towards Evil Sister. Evil Sister dodges and right hooks Black Lotus in her rib, then elbows her in the back, dropping her to the ground.

"You seem lost. How about I help you out there?" Evil Sister says while picking Black Lotus up and throwing her across the way.

"What did you do with them?" Black Lotus says while getting up.

"I don't recall," Evil Sister says, running towards Black Lotus. Black Lotus stomps on her right foot again, and the blade shoots out. Black Lotus kicks Evil Sister in the knee, slicing through her leg. Evil

Sister drops to her knees, struggling to get back on her feet.

Black Lotus then stabs Evil Sister in her stomach, saying, "Now why don't you tell me, or do I need to keep slashing through your body?"

Evil Sister smirks, then chuckles and says, "Well, this was fun, but it's only the beginning."

A grenade drops out of her hands, forcing Black Lotus to let go of Evil Sister and leap for cover.

"You'll never find your friends; I'll kill them before you do!" Evil Sister runs toward a cliff and jumps off right into a helicopter, to her inevitable escape.

"Fuck, fuck, fuck!!!" Black Lotus runs out to the loading docks to find her speedboat.

"I need to get to land," Black Lotus thinks to herself. She hops on the speedboat and rides off to shore.

An hour later

Once Mazikeen gets to shore, she finds herself near a road. Mazikeen runs into the middle of the road and jumps in front of a car to stop it.

"Get out!" Mazikeen yells. The guy gets out of the car, confused, and Mazikeen gets in. Mazikeen is making her way to save her only friends.

On Mazikeen's way to the safe house, where

she knows Evil Sister is holding her friend captive, Mazikeen gets a call; it's Evil Sister.

"You better hurry, you don't want to miss the bloodbath."

"This evil, conniving bitch!" Mazikeen skirts around the corner and drives the car into the safe house, barely missing her friends.

"Mazikeen!" Scarlet and Ash yell.

"Now listen here, you do not touch my friends. They're off-limits," Mazikeen says, unwavering.

"Oh, is that so? Show me then," Evil Sister says tauntingly. Evil Sister and Mazikeen begin sparring.

In the middle of their fight, Evil Sister says, "Do you remember when you were first adopted? Do you remember when you got your name, Black Lotus?"

"What does that have to do with anything?" Mazikeen asks, lunging backwards to avoid the strike.

"I took you under my wing when they decided to adopt you, taught you everything you know," Evil Sister says, frustratedly, after slashing Mazikeen on her right cheek.

"Mother took me under her wing. She taught me." Mazikeen touches her face angrily, then rushes to finish her attack.

"No, Mother didn't teach you, I did," Evil Sister

says gloatingly.

"You were better than me at the age of 12, do you know how that makes me look?" Evil Sister cries out, landing another hit on Mazikeen.

"I thought no way our little Black Lotus can exceed me..." Mazikeen pierces Evil Sister in her shoulder. Mazikeen then smashes Evil Sister's face upon her knee, throwing her back into a daze.

"My #1 spot!" Evil Sister huffs, finishing what she was trying to say. "It's like I didn't matter anymore!"

Evil Sister leaps towards Mazikeen; Mazikeen sweeps her off Her Feet and drops her to the floor.

"Ugh!!" she says. Mazikeen stands on top of her; she presses her blade to Dreux's throat, her chest heaving.

"All this time, you thought power meant silence. But emotion is strength. Family is strength." Mazikeen doesn't flinch as her blade cuts. Dreux's chapter ends the same way it began, with Mazikeen refusing to break.

"Look at that, little Lotus all grown up..." Evil Sister says gaspingly with her last breath, then dies.

"Goodbye, Dreux." Mazikeen takes a moment and walks towards her friends to unite with them.

"Let's go home, guys," Mazikeen says with a sigh of relief.

Back to Reality

5 years later

Mazikeen is now 23 years old and in college with Scarlet and Ash; everything is finally back to the way it was. Mazikeen doesn't have to watch her every step; life is good for them.

"Let's get ice cream, I'm craving a Rocky Road!" Scarlet says with stars in her eyes.

"Yeah!" Ash says, leaning on Mazikeen.

"Fine, I'll drive," Mazikeen laughs. They get to the ice cream shop, and everyone gets the ice cream they want.

"Sit outside?" Ash asks. The girls nod. They sit down talking about all their classes and upcoming exams, laughing and joking around.

Mazikeen sits back and thinks to herself, "I'm the luckiest girl in the world right now," and Mazikeen intends to protect it, but for now, she lets herself enjoy it, even knowing the peace never lasts forever. However, Mazikeen knows the Head Councilman and Father are still out there somewhere, and she will be ready.

NOTE FROM THE AUTHOR

1. Will Mazikeen keep Scarlet and Ash out of the dangerous trouble that might be coming her way this time?

2. Will Mazikeen take down The Red Veil Organization?

3. Was Mazikeen safe after all, or will The Red Veil organization and Father be coming back for her sooner than later?

Find out in the 2nd book, Undercover Assassin 2: The Plans That Stop the World.